# FRANZESKA G. EWART

# Bryony Bell's Star Turn

## Illustrated by Kelly Waldek

**A & C Black • London**

*To Louise and Emma Fagan*

First published 2005 by
A & C Black Publishers Ltd
37 Soho Square, London, W1D 3QZ

www.acblack.com

Text copyright © 2005 Franzeska G. Ewart
Illustrations copyright © 2005 Kelly Waldek

The excerpt from 'When You Wish Upon A Star'
(Washington/Harline) which appears on page 62 is used
with the kind permission of Bourne Music Ltd

The rights of Franzeska G. Ewart and Kelly Waldek to be
identified as the author and illustrator of this work respectively
have been asserted by them in accordance with the
Copyrights, Designs and Patents Act 1988.

ISBN-10: 0-7136-7171-8
ISBN-13: 978-0-7136-7171-1

A CIP catalogue for this book is available from the British Library.

A & C Black uses paper produced with elemental chlorine-free
pulp, harvested from managed sustained forests.

Printed and bound in Great Britain by Bookmarque Ltd, Croydon

# Chapter One

Bryony Bell beamed at the gold shooting star she had just stuck on her bedroom door, and the gold shooting star beamed back.

'Got it at last,' she whispered, skating past all the other star-studded bedroom doors. 'And what's more,' she added, '*my* star is set to shoot higher and higher and *higher*!'

She spread her arms wide, bent her knees, and launched herself into a quadruple jump, doing the splits as she landed. Then she bent down so her forehead touched her knees and, for a moment, relived the rapturous applause *Ashraf and Bell – Magic on Wheels* had received during their mega-successful week on Broadway at the end of that summer.

They hadn't been the only magic act on the bill. They'd shared the stage with Ken Undrum (Man of Mystery, and Bryony and Abid's manager) and his brother, The Great Ronaldo.

The once-popular magician brothers had made a comeback, with their spectacular illusions proving as popular as ever. People had clamoured for tickets, night after triumphant night.

But, breathtaking though Ken and Ronaldo were, it was *Ashraf and Bell* who had stolen the show. Audiences had sat riveted as Abid's soprano voice belted out magic spells with gusto, and each time a baby rabbit appeared from a hat, or an egg was produced from an ear, they had stamped their feet and yelled for more. Never, in the history of magic acts, had there been *such* a glamorous assistant as Bryony Bell. Everyone had gazed spellbound as she glided round the stage, a vision of sparkling-white loveliness on her glistening Viper 3000 rollerskates, making sure every trick was performed with the utmost slickness. And when finally Abid sawed Bryony in half, you would have thought the theatre's gilded walls would burst.

Bryony sighed at the memory. It had been *perfect*.

No, she corrected herself as she walked thoughtfully downstairs, not perfect. For after every performance, when she and Abid had bowed to the audience, one face was always missing. One face, half hidden by a big red handkerchief. One face, its blue eyes glowing more brightly with pride than any other.

'It's just not the same,' Bryony had confided in Abid, 'when your dad's not there to see you.'

Abid had agreed. But for Abid it was different. *His* father hadn't been in New York because he was a doctor and was too busy to get away. But Big Bob would never *ever* see Bryony perform in the States. The mere thought of flying brought him out in a cold sweat. No matter how she cajoled and wheedled and begged, Bryony knew she would never get him on a plane.

The *Singing Bells* had made their Broadway debut too. In an even grander theatre one block away, Bryony's mum, Clarissa Bell, and her sisters Angelina, Melody, Melissa and Emmy-Lou, with Little Bob on drums, wowed audiences with their gutsy musical version of *Cinderella*.

*Angelina Bell's performance as Fairy Godmother*, the *New York Times* had announced, under the headline BROADWAY APPLAUDS THE BELLES, *was the icing on the glitziest cake in New York*.

Clarissa was over the moon when she saw it. 'Look how they've spelt us, kids!' she said, pointing to the 'e' at the end of 'Belle'. 'We all know what "belle" means, don't we?'

Then she explained that it meant a 'beautiful young lady', and Angelina and Melody and Melissa and Emmy-Lou squirmed with delight and rushed off to buy more lip gloss and blusher.

And so the *Singing Bells* had become the *Broadway Belles* and, having achieved their dream of performing on Broadway, were now more determined than ever to 'make it big' in the USA.

The kitchen reflected their ambitions. A large Stars and Stripes flag covered one wall, and the rest were stuck with posters, photographs and other memorabilia. A stuffed bear's head, which had been a gift from one of Clarissa's adoring fans, took pride of place. The bear sported a white rhinestone-studded Stetson, which had been a gift from another adoring fan, and the combined effect was extremely impressive, if a little sinister.

There was no doubt, Bryony reflected as she skated into the kitchen, that the week on Broadway had changed everyone's lives for the better. Hadn't it? She tipped a load of potatoes into the sink and began to peel, pausing from time to time to stare into their little brown eyes.

The trouble was, she thought for the millionth time, that now the Belles had experienced the thrill of Broadway, they'd be sure to want a whole summer season at the very least. And, though Bryony was as keen as the rest of them to be a big transatlantic starlet, she just hated the thought of leaving Big Bob behind all that time.

'Mum's bound to want me and Abid to go,' Bryony explained to a particularly sympathetic-looking King Edward, 'because she wants us *all* to be mega-famous.

'And Mr Undrum'll want us to go because we make his magic act even better,' she went on, paring the potato's skin off rather savagely.

'And Abid's mum's just *dying* for us to go so she can come along and be Designer to the Stars,' she added, gouging out two of its eyes.

'So,' she said, slicing it decisively in half, 'it's just as well that Yours Truly has a breathtakingly brilliant, scintillatingly sure-fire gem of an idea up her sleeve.'

She plopped the potato pieces into the pot and viewed them with satisfaction. 'It's a bit of a long shot,' she said confidentially, putting on the lid. 'But then, breathtakingly brilliant, scintillatingly sure-fire gems of ideas tend to be…'

Bryony waited till the potatoes were boiling, then skated up the frosty moonlit path to the music studio, where the *Broadway Belles* were still practising. She gritted her teeth as Little Bob's drum announced the beginning of the latest Belle Family Song.

'*We're the BROADWAY BELLES*
*And we've hit the highest heights*
*We're the BROADWAY BELLES*
*And our names are up in lights*
*But the BROADWAY BELLES*
*Have a greater dream by far…*'

Bryony stopped, hand on the door, and braced herself for the next lines.

'*…For in Ho-lly-wood,*' they sang, Little Bob emphasising the last three syllables with loud *booms!*

'*Where? In HO-LLY-WOOD?*' they continued, the drumbeats rising to an ear-shattering crescendo.

'*Yes! In HO-LLY-WOOD,*' they answered themselves, even more deafeningly.

'*WE'RE GONNA STAR!*'

'Rats!' Bryony muttered, slipping into the

**10**

humid warmth of the studio. 'No change there, then.'

Each Broadway Belle held two fluorescent-pink pompoms and as Bryony glided in they launched, quite suddenly and unexpectedly, into a frenzy of waving and jumping up and down.

'*HO-LLY-WOOD!*' they roared.

'*HO-LLY-WOOD!*'

'*RA! RA! RA!*'

'Take five!' Clarissa yelled above the racket, and everyone except Little Bob dropped their pompoms, rushed over to their vanity cases, and began to reapply eye shadow and lip gloss as if there were no tomorrow.

'Don't you think the little 'uns are getting a bit *too* obsessed with their looks?' Bryony whispered to Clarissa. 'I mean to say, it's just a singing practice.'

Clarissa examined her Cranberry Crystal fingernails. 'You never know the hour, Bryony,' she said mysteriously.

'How do you mean, Mum?'

Clarissa peered over her sunglasses. 'Film producers, of course!' she replied. 'You mark my words – our Angelina's acting's the talk of the town. Any day now that door'll open and there they'll be, pleading with us to sign their Hollywood contracts. Pleading,' she repeated, spraying three blasts of *L'Air du Temps* into her cleavage. 'And maybe, Bryony,' she added, 'there'll be a film with a skating part for you. Mmm?'

'That'd be great, Mum,' Bryony agreed. 'Though not terribly likely…' she added under her breath.

'Just came to say the potatoes are on,' she continued more cheerfully. 'Mr Undrum's coming, remember?' She looked around to see that Angelina was out of earshot. 'Said he'd show me a spot of hypnosis once my tea's down,' she whispered. 'Only don't tell Angelina, 'cause of you-know-what…'

Clarissa nodded. 'Mum's the word!' she whispered. Then, keeping her voice low, she went on. 'Rather odd, don't you think, that Ken decided to come back to stay with Abid's family again?'

'Very odd,' Bryony nodded, 'considering things were going so well on Broadway. Still, Mr Undrum *is* a Man of Mystery.'

'Moves in mysterious ways, Bryony,' Clarissa agreed. 'And there ain't nothing like a Man of Mystery,' she said as she pulled on her strawberry-pink, crushed-velvet cloak and led the way out into the snow, 'to add zest to your bangers and mash.'

As everyone tumbled into the kitchen, Bryony checked the potatoes and laid out the sausages. As she pricked them, she thought again about her breathtakingly brilliant, scintillatingly sure-fire gem of an idea.

A few weeks earlier, after an enormous amount of thought and without telling a living soul, she had written a very, very important letter. It had, Bryony reflected, been extremely hard to decide what to write, and even harder to decide how to spell it. But she had managed and, she thought with satisfaction, no one could deny it was a real cracker of a letter! If that letter didn't change the *Broadway Belles* back into nice, stay-at-home *Singing Bells*, Bryony thought, nothing would and it might even meet with Angelina's approval.

At the thought of Angelina, Bryony's spirits sank. 'Angelina's approval' – never the most plentiful commodity – was in particularly short supply these days.

It wasn't that Bryony hadn't tried ever so hard to be nice. Hadn't she chosen the sweetest, most delectable of Lily the rabbit's thirteen babies to give Angelina as a present? And didn't she bend over backwards to keep it supplied with tasty titbits, even spending her own pocket money now Big Bob's vegetable patch had run out? Without a doubt, looking after little Starburst together had improved things between them for a while.

And if it hadn't been for Mr Undrum's onion, Bryony thought, they might still be getting on. Well, not just Mr Undrum's onion, actually. There was also the dreaded school Nativity play… Bryony gave herself a shake. She must not not *not* think about the school Nativity play. It was simply too awful for words.

Suddenly an ear-splitting 'Hiya, kids!' told her that Ken Undrum had arrived.

Sliding the sausages under the grill, Bryony raced to the front door, flung herself into his arms, and gazed into his bright, blackberry eyes. 'Stage hypnotism tonight, Mr Undrum?' she whispered, hoping he hadn't forgotten his promise.

And, of course, he hadn't. His red handlebar moustache quivered as he nodded his shock of flame-coloured hair. 'Gee, Bryony honey!' he replied. 'Didn'tcha just read my mind!'

# Chapter Two

Mrs Quigg, the music teacher, whirled round on the piano stool and surveyed the stage disapprovingly over her half-moon spectacles.

'*Do* stop fidgeting, Angelina,' she said. 'And try to look a bit more like the Multitude of the Heavenly Host, could you?'

Angelina peered morosely out through her braids. 'It's quite hard, Mrs Quigg,' she pointed out, 'when there's only me, and one of my wings is loose.'

Mrs Quigg dragged her hands through her hair, dislodging several hairpins. 'It's called "stage presence", dear,' she said. 'And if you want to be a proper actor you'll have to develop some.'

Sitting on a bench beside Abid, Bryony watched their class teacher march over to Angelina and tug the string round her waist.

'There we are,' Mrs Ogilvie said, giving her a shake. 'Solid as the Walls of Jericho.'

Mrs Quigg raised her eyebrows heavenwards, then she ran her fingers lightly up and down the piano keys. 'I composed this,' she explained to Angelina, 'to sound like the flutter of angel's wings. So please do not forget it is your cue to flap and sing.'

She glared over to where Bryony was sitting. 'And when the Virgin Mary sees the Multitude of the Heavenly Host,' she added, 'she gives them her full attention – *doesn't* she?'

Bryony leapt to her feet, adjusted the tea towel round her head, and shuffled forward.

'OK, Angelina,' said Mrs Quigg. '*Behold, I bring you great good news*! And make sure you sound the final consonants, otherwise it sounds like "grey goo"…'

It was the second week of rehearsals and already everyone was feeling the strain. Mrs Quigg, spurred on by the success of her *Ugly Duckling* that summer, had written another musical which, she had announced confidently, was a *tour de force* to end all *tour de forces*.

The words *tour de force* had brought Abid out in a rash, but when Mrs Quigg had told him he was to be Joseph he had gulped, wheezed deeply, and assured her he would give it his best shot.

**17**

The only remaining thing the play needed, Mrs Quigg had told the cast, was a show-stopping Big Number. But when they had asked what the Big Number actually *was*, she had blushed and explained that the muse had not yet descended but that she was expecting an imminent visitation.

'We are talking about the mystery of artistic inspiration,' she had explained solemnly. 'One simply cannot rush these things.'

As the days passed, however, and no artistic inspiration was forthcoming, Mrs Quigg's mood had darkened. She frequently burst into tears, and not even Angelina's angelic voice could lift her spirits. Rehearsals were a nightmare.

Quite apart from sympathising with Mrs Quigg's battle with the muse, Bryony had her own private misgivings about the Nativity play. OK – she was the star, and that was as it should be. But when you looked at what an angel got to wear (layers of sequined white chiffon, a diamond tiara, and enormous gold-foil-covered cardboard wings), compared to the Virgin Mary (two tea towels, a sheet, and a grey shawl with a pillow stuffed underneath), there was no doubt which part *she'd* rather play.

Bryony gazed enviously at Angelina while Angelina sang the Angel song as sweetly as ever. Secretly, she slipped her hand underneath her shawl and felt inside her pocket. A tingle of excitement ran up her spine. The reply to her letter – and *exactly* what she had hoped for! She had hardly had time to take it in, let alone show it to Abid. She couldn't wait for playtime to come.

'Superb, Angelina!' Mrs Quigg beamed up at Angelina as the last notes tinkled away. Then she glared at Bryony. 'Bryony Bell,' she growled. 'An angel has just appeared to tell you that you are going to be the mother of the son of God, and you stand there looking like a cauliflower. Now *think*! How will that joyful news make you *feel*?'

Bryony tugged at her tea towel and glanced over to where Abid was standing tugging at his. He mouthed something. Bryony narrowed her eyes, then turned back to Mrs Quigg.

'Pleased?' she said hopefully.

'*Pleased*?' repeated Mrs Quigg. It was clearly not the correct answer. 'Is that *all*?'

Bryony looked over at Abid again; but Abid shrugged his shoulders.

'Very pleased?' she tried miserably.

'Oh, honestly!' shrieked Mrs Quigg. 'Surely *you*, coming from a show-biz family, can think of something a tad more powerful than "very pleased"?'

Out of the corner of her eye, Bryony could see Angelina putting her hand up. She had a more than usually self-satisfied expression on her face.

'Yes, Angelina?' Mrs Quigg said expectantly.

'If *I* were playing the Virgin Mary, Mrs Quigg,' Angelina replied in her most simpering voice, '*I* should be filled with the utmost awe.'

'Awe,' Mrs Quigg repeated, rolling the word around her mouth. 'Awe,' she repeated, savouring it. Then she glared back at Bryony. 'Exactly!' she barked. 'A little more *awe* from the Virgin Mary, or she's going to end up losing her star part.'

At that, much to Bryony's relief, the bell rang. As everyone threw off their tea towels, she pulled Abid impatiently towards the classroom. 'Just wait till you see this!' she hissed.

'It's not that book about hypnosis you got from Mr Undrum last night?' Abid looked worried. 'Only I can't cope with much more today.' He sank down onto a chair and put his head in his hands. 'Oh, Bryony,' he said miserably. 'I do *hate* being an actor!'

Bryony sat down beside him. 'You used to hate singing in public,' she observed. 'And there you were a couple of months ago, wowing half the States.'

'That was different,' Abid sighed. 'That was singing. It's all this *acting* I can't stand. I just hate it when I have to gaze at you, my eyes filled with a mixture of love and compassion, and say, "Not much longer, my darling. Behold I see the star ahead",'

'You do it very movingly,' Bryony pointed out. 'And it means the world to Mrs Quigg.'

'I know it means the world to Mrs Quigg,' Abid agreed. 'But it's more than I can stand.'

Bryony concealed a sigh. 'Think yourself lucky you can sing,' she said impatiently. '*I* have to act all the flipping time because I *can't*. And all *I* want to do is skate.'

Then, to Abid's surprise, she leapt onto a desk, pulled an envelope from her pocket, and took two pieces of paper out of it. 'But it is time to forget your sorrows,' she announced, unfolding the top piece of paper, 'for behold I bring you glad tidings of great joy! From the Director of Channel 4, no less – so pin back your ears.

'*Dear Ms Bell*,' she read, as Abid gazed open-mouthed. '*Thank you for your letter. After due consideration, we have great pleasure in taking up your proposal to make a docu-soap of life with the Bells.*

'*As you suggest, we will install a film crew to follow your family throughout the coming twelve months.*

'*Time being of the essence, if we are to have a Christmas special, we would wish to begin screen tests immediately. We trust this meets with your parents' approval.*

'*We enclose a contract, the terms of which we are confident will be satisfactory.*'

Bryony unfolded the second piece of paper and waved the contract in front of Abid. 'Feast your eyes on *this*!' she said. 'Enough to keep the *Broadway Belles* grounded for at least a year, don't you think?'

Abid stared, blinked, and stared again. 'All that money…' he breathed, '…and fame too. Oh, Bryony, you're a genius!'

He stood up and applauded Bryony, who curtsied. Just as she was surfacing, Mrs Ogilvie entered the classroom. Bryony braced herself for the backlash, but amazingly none came. Instead, Mrs Ogilvie merely raised her eyebrows.

'Might I make so bold as to suggest,' she commented, as she swept past with a pile of spelling books, 'that we do not let our Nativity play parts go *quite* so much to our heads?'

# Chapter Three

When Bryony finished reading the letter from Channel 4 to Big Bob, Clarissa, and the little Bells, the kitchen fell silent. Then everyone spoke at once.

'We've *nothing* to wear!'

'We'll need complete makeovers!'

'And personal trainers!'

'And image consultants!'

Struggling to make herself heard over the list of requirements, Clarissa announced:

'Three cheers for Bryony!' And, when these had been duly delivered, rather spoilt the effect for Bryony by adding, '*Now* we'll be head-hunted for Hollywood, nothing surer.'

When everyone had calmed down, Bryony edged closer to Big Bob, who was quietly tightening the screws around the stuffed bear's head. 'What do you think, Dad?' she whispered nervously. 'Be good for *Bell's Building 'n' Joinery*, won't it?'

'Ever so good, Bryony love,' Big Bob assured her. 'Specially if we get close-ups of my dovetail joints and my French polishing.'

Clarissa, meanwhile, was rounding up the little Bells with some difficulty. 'Off to the music studio!' she said, knotting Little Bob's scarf. 'Mustn't let this excitement keep us away from our daily practice.'

When they had disappeared, Bryony hopped up onto the table and leant her head against Big Bob's shoulder. '*Sure* you like the idea of a docu-soap, Dad?' she said anxiously. 'I kind of wondered whether you'd think it was a bit…' She struggled to find the right word.

'Tacky?' Big Bob suggested.

'Oh, Dad…' She bit her lip. 'You *don't* think it's tacky, do you?'

But Big Bob merely gave each screw a final turn. 'Safe as houses,' he grinned, giving the head a tug. 'Wouldn't do if it fell on us in front of the great British public, would it!'

Bryony grinned back. 'Anyway,' she said, 'the docu-soap'll keep them at home for a bit, won't it?' and to her relief, Big Bob nodded.

'Take the "e" out of "Belle",' he agreed

thoughtfully. Then he propped his screwdriver behind his ear, smoothed his moustache, and beamed at her, first in one direction and then in the other. 'What do you think, lass?' he asked. 'Which is my best side?'

When the film crew arrived a week later and Bryony saw Trish the producer, she thought she had never, in all her born days, met anyone so right-on cool.

Trish was coat-hanger thin and even taller than Abid. Her hair was very short and blonde except for an orange crest down the middle. Her enormous green eyes shone like stars in an eye-shadowy black sky. Her smile would have been sparkly even without the red jewel shimmering from the piercing in her top lip, and her hooped earrings were so big, each could have fitted round her neck.

She wore an extremely tight T-shirt and extremely baggy combat trousers covered in pockets out of which spilled an incredible array of useful objects like elastic bands, scissors, and measuring tapes; and she carried a clipboard.

'I was thinking,' Clarissa said as she led Trish, two heavily laden cameramen and a sound engineer into the living room, 'that perhaps you could film me ever so slightly out of focus?

'With a pink *aura* round my head,' she added, sinking down onto the settee and adjusting her white silk housecoat. 'Mmm?'

Trish closed one eye, looked Clarissa up and down, and made some notes on her clipboard. 'Wicked,' she muttered several times. 'Though I think lilac for the aura, if you're OK with that?' And she began to check her cast list.

'My husband is in his potting shed,' Clarissa explained apologetically. 'But he is available for interview whenever you want.'

'Fabulous,' said Trish. 'Now, here's what's gonna happen,' she went on, in a business-like voice. 'The show'll be filmed at half-past seven every morning. Live action'll be interspersed with highlights of key events from the day before, plus outside-broadcast specials.' She gave each Bell a piercing stare. 'Questions?'

Angelina raised a nervous hand. 'Did you say "half-past seven every morning"?' she repeated, aghast.

'Sure!' Trish answered brightly. 'Yeah, I know, it's kinda early and I *had* hoped for tea time, but that's what the bosses want. "Revolutionise the nation's breakfast time, Trish", they told me.' She took out a digital camera. 'And that,' she went on, aiming it at the Bells, 'is exactly what I intend to do. Now – publicity photos!'

The little 'uns, who had spent the previous week choosing make-up and clothes and thinking about their images, immediately cheered up and struck a variety of poses. Angelina had gone for a moody and mysterious look and did some magnificent close-up pouts through her braids. Melody and Melissa had dressed identically, with the same spiky gel-glistened hairstyle, in a bid to confuse the viewers. Emmy-

Lou had so many lacy petticoats on she looked like a tiny tap-dancing powder puff, and Little Bob, resplendent in Bob the Builder T-shirt, shorts, safety helmet and yellow plastic hammer, gave charming, if toothless, smiles to the camera as he fixed everything in sight.

But when it was Bryony's turn to be photographed, everyone else faded into insignificance.

'*Awe*some, Bryony!' Trish gasped as Bryony glided across the carpet and did three spins and a triple jump. 'Your skating's gonna give the show such a *lift*!'

Bryony beamed happily and assured Trish that if it was a 'lift' she was wanting, she'd come to the right place.

'You see what a talented family I have,' Clarissa said proudly. 'Now – how about a cup of tea?' And she led Trish into the kitchen.

The moment Trish stepped inside the room, she lost all powers of speech. Open-mouthed, she gazed at the enormous Stars and Stripes flag. Letting out a low whistle, she took in the publicity posters. And when she saw the stuffed bear's head with its rhinestone-studded Stetson, her joy knew no bounds.

'What a wicked kitchen!' she breathed at last. 'A photo opportunity to end all photo opportunities!'

She scribbled on her clipboard like a thing possessed, then beamed at the Bells. 'This location,' she told them ecstatically, 'is the inspiration I needed.'

'I see it all now,' she went on dreamily. 'We call the show Breakfast with the Bells and we open with speeded-up shots of each of you bursting through the kitchen door. There'll be a bit of chat, live from the breakfast table, then we'll cut to recorded highlights and Star Interviews, then back for more chat.' She flung her arms round Clarissa's neck, gave her two large kisses, and sighed. 'It'll be something else!'

'The breakfast show with *style*,' Clarissa agreed, then suddenly drew herself up to her full height. 'I believe,' she said importantly, 'inspiration has also struck *me*. If you will excuse us, Trish, we'll leave you in Bryony's capable hands to have that cup of tea.'

She motioned towards the door and waited as the little 'uns obediently formed a line. 'Off to the music studio, *Broadway Belles*!' she announced. 'I feel a Big Number coming on

**30**

that'll put a bang into the nation's snap, crackle and pop!'

# Chapter Four

Trish had decided that the first Breakfast with the Bells screen test should take place on Saturday, so that school didn't interfere with the action.

So, bright and early that morning, the Bells excitedly put on their make-up and best outfits, and assembled outside the kitchen. Each member of the *Broadway Belles* had two fluorescent-pink pompoms and Little Bob had his hammer, onto which two tiny pompoms had been tied.

Trish inspected everyone and nodded approvingly. '*Adore* the pompoms,' she said.

'We wondered,' Clarissa began tentatively, 'whether we might run my latest Big Number past you? I thought it might do as a theme tune.'

Trish's face lit up. 'Triffic!' she said. 'We'll record it, and use it to practise the opening titles.'

As Clarissa lined up the *Broadway Belles*, Trish

gave the sound engineer his instructions. Angelina, Melody, Melissa and Emmy-Lou stood in a neat row in front of the Stars and Stripes wall, while Little Bob sat on the draining board, hammer poised. As Clarissa pointed her conductor's baton at him, he gave its metal surface three ear-splitting bangs.

Then, taking a line each and raising their pompoms as they sang, the Bell sisters belted out Clarissa's Big Number:

*'We'll put the "sun" into sunny-side-up!*
*We'll charm the tea right out of the cup!*
*We'll add a bang! to your snap, crackle and pop!*
*We'll make you wish your breakfast time would…*
*… ne … ver … stop!'*

At this line they all joined in and sang very slowly, sinking down on one knee and swivelling round to face Little Bob, who obligingly banged his hammer another three times.

Then everyone jumped to their feet, gripped each other round the waist and, with a series of breathtakingly high kicks, advanced towards Trish and, their smiles fairly dazzling her, finished the song perched atop the kitchen table:

*'So start the day the bell-shaped way*
*It's sure to make you smile*
*And have your breakfast with the Bells –*
*The breakfast show with style!'*

'Wicked!' Trish cheered. 'Now, Clarissa,' she went on excitedly, 'would you be so kind as to fetch your husband from the potting shed? I think the oldest should burst through first.'

All morning the Bells launched themselves into the opening titles with gusto, and by lunch time the sequence was almost ready for a final take.

'Perhaps not *quite* so much of a pout,' Trish suggested tentatively to Angelina. 'Don't want to put the nation off its Sunny Delight, do we?'

As Angelina drew in breath to argue her case, the doorbell chimed out a tinny chorus of *ding! dong! merrily on high!* With some relief, Bryony glided off to open the door. And when she saw who it was, she could not have been more pleased.

'Trish,' she announced proudly, leading the visitors into the kitchen, 'this is Mr Ken Undrum, and his star pupil, Abid Ashraf.'

Giving up for the moment on Angelina, whose pout had deepened with Ken's arrival, Trish stood up and shook their hands. 'Ken Undrum, Man of Mystery,' she breathed in reverential tones. 'Bryony's told me all about you and your incredible powers. You know I'm on the lookout for someone to be our first Star Interview?' she went on, as Angelina flounced out of the kitchen. 'How about it, Mr Undrum?'

Without a moment's hesitation Ken nodded. 'Sure thing!' he said, rubbing his hands together enthusiastically. 'Oh boy, could I tell you some stories about the old Broadway days! Come to think of it,' he winked towards Bryony and Abid, 'I gorra few tricks up my sleeve right now. Care to be astounded?'

Bryony and Abid watched anxiously as he withdrew a length of gold chain from which dangled a bright, sparkling crystal.

'Don't worry, Bryony,' Abid whispered. 'Angelina's upstairs.'

'Look into the crystal,' Ken told Trish in a low-pitched monotonous voice. He swung the pendulum back and forth, and everyone watched in silence as Trish's eyes grew more and more glazed. 'Now,' Ken said, 'clasp your hands.'

Obediently, Trish did as she was told. Everyone gasped. Melody and Melissa clung together, and Clarissa hugged Emmy-Lou close, patted Little Bob on the head, and assured them that Mr Undrum was only having a bit of fun.

'I will begin to count,' Ken went on dramatically, 'and when I reach three you will be wide awake. But whenever you hear the word "bell", your hands will once more glue themselves together and will remain locked until you hear the word again.

'One … two … three…'

At the last number, Ken snapped his fingers.

Trish was instantly wide awake. 'So why did you come back to England with the Bells, Mr Undrum?' she asked. Instantly, her hands clamped together. 'Did you think you'd miss them too much?' Trish stared wildly at her whitening knuckles. 'The Bells, I mean,' she went on, giving a little cry as once more her hands loosened.

Bryony and Abid waited with bated breath for Ken Undrum's reply. This was exactly the question *they* had been longing to ask.

'Affairs of the heart, Trish, my dear,' he said, slipping the crystal back in his pocket and giving it a pat. 'Although, of course,' he continued, winking mischievously at his audience, 'I'm always happy to be with the Bells!'

No sooner was the word out, than Trish's hands clamped together yet again. And just as they did, the kitchen door was thrown open and there, wearing her biggest pout to date, stood Angelina, hands indignantly on hips.

'You've let yourself fall under Mr Undrum's power,' she told Trish in a low and ominous voice. 'Just like I did!' She pointed an accusing finger at Ken, then wheeled round to include Bryony and Abid. 'This magic act can not be trusted!' she announced, and as Trish looked in horror at the three mortified magicians, Angelina, shaking with fury, explained. 'They made me *eat an onion*,' she said dramatically. 'On *Broadway*!'

There was a stunned silence, then Ken spoke. 'Oh gee, Angelina honey,' he said, 'I told you a hundred times I was sorry. Can't you let bygones be bygones?'

But one look at Angelina's face made it abundantly clear that letting bygones be bygones was the last thing on her mind. She took in a deep breath, then erupted again.

'Of course, I lay most of the blame,' she shrieked, 'on the *glamorous assistant*!' And she marched up to Bryony. 'The *glamorous assistant* who got me up on stage,' she continued, pushing her face so close to Bryony's that the beads of her braids dug into her cheeks, 'and very nearly *poisoned* me…'

Suddenly it was more than Bryony could bear. 'It was only an onion, for goodness' sake,' she said reasonably. 'And you thought it was an apple, so it couldn't have been *that* bad.'

The air in the packed kitchen was heady with emotion as the two sisters faced one another.

'You *promised* you wouldn't let Mr Undrum do any more hypnotism!' Anglina shouted almost incoherently. 'It's *ruining* our screen test!'

'But, Angelina...' Bryony began, then stopped. It was useless.

'*Every* time it looks as though our singing act's going to get somewhere,' Angelina screeched on, 'you and your Mr Undrum find a way to stop us. Jealous of our success, that's what you are!'

'Now, now, Angelina,' Clarissa said in her most soothing voice. 'You're exaggerating, dear.'

But nothing was going to soothe Angelina. 'I'm *not*,' she sobbed. 'And it's high time the whole British nation knew what a snake in the grass Bryony Bell is!' She spun round and, with great diginity, made her way to the back door where she turned to face her dumbstruck audience. 'I wish no further communication with you, Bryony,' she announced in a voice tremulous with emotion. 'This is the straw that has broken the camel's back.' She paused to wipe her eyes with one of her braids. 'Henceforth,' she concluded, 'I will provide Starburst's vegetation

**39**

without your help.'

And, in the stunned silence that followed, she made her exit.

That afternoon, the air in the Bell house was electric with tension. Trish had decided that everyone's nerves were too frayed to continue rehearsals and had left with her camera crew. Clarissa and Big Bob had made Ken a cup of extra-strong coffee and, along with the little Bells, were doing their best to comfort him in the living room. Angelina was sulking in her bedroom.

Bryony and Abid leant against Bryony's wardrobe, munching chocolate digestive biscuits and washing them down with cocoa. At last Abid drained his mug and set it down carefully on the pink shag-pile carpet.

'Wouldn't think you could get that much raw emotion into one kitchen, would you?' he observed.

'Best tantrum to date,' Bryony agreed. 'Thank goodness we weren't on air!' She ran her hands through the shag pile. 'Hope she doesn't keep starting fights when we're filming, even if it *does* make great television…'

She hoisted herself to her feet. 'I just don't see *what* I can do to make Angelina feel better about me,' she said, skating a dismal circuit of the bedroom. 'I can't believe that I'm even denied visiting rights to poor old Starburst!'

Abid solemnly watched Bryony, racking his brains for something comforting to say. Finally he gave up and changed the subject. 'I thought for a minute Mr Undrum was going to tell Trish why he came back to England,' he said.

'Clammed up, as usual,' Bryony agreed. 'He's a hard nut to crack.'

Abid hesitated. 'I've got a bit of a clue though,' he said slowly. 'About the affair of the heart...'

'A clue?' Bryony brightened up.

'A *heart-shaped* clue,' Abid said, mysteriously.

'Come on then,' Bryony said, kneeling down and thumping his knees with her fists. 'Spit it out!'

'It was last night, when I took him his malted milk,' Abid said slowly. 'I saw him shove something under his pillow. Then this morning it was on his bedside table, and I got a good look.'

'So...' Bryony urged. 'What was it?'

'A picture of a woman,' Abid whispered excitedly. 'In a gold, heart-shaped frame.'

'A love interest!' Bryony gasped. 'Was she exquisitely beautiful, Abid?'

'A vision of loveliness,' Abid replied. 'Long, wavy, red hair, rosy cheeks and a very alluring smile. For a moment I thought—'

'Abid!' Clarissa was calling from downstairs. 'Mr Undrum's ready to go!'

Abid pulled himself up.

'What did you think for a moment?' Bryony asked impatiently, as she followed him downstairs.

'Oh…' shrugged Abid. 'Nothing really.'

Bryony unhooked Ken's coat and scarf from the stand and began to open the living room door. 'Tell me anyway?' she pleaded.

'Well…' Abid said doubtfully. 'The vision of loveliness reminded me of someone.'

'Who?' gasped Bryony.

'Just a little…' Abid added cautiously.

'*Who?*' Bryony repeated.

'Probably just a trick of the light,' Abid answered dismissively. 'The picture's very faded.'

But Bryony's mind was racing. 'Someone I know too?' she asked.

Abid nodded, but before he could say any more, Clarissa led Ken gently out into the hall and took his coat and scarf from Bryony.

'All this stardom,' Clarissa said apologetically as she helped Ken into his coat, 'has made our Angelina forget her manners. There will be strong words later, I promise.'

'No, no, dear lady,' Ken said, shaking his head mournfully. 'It is I who am entirely to blame.'

Clarissa opened the front door. A little flurry of snowflakes swirled into the hall.

'Do please assure Angelina,' Ken went on, as Abid joined him on the doorstep, 'that I have hung up my onions forever.'

Bryony squeezed past Clarissa. 'I won't get a wink of sleep if you don't tell me,' she hissed desperately in Abid's ear. 'Someone at school?'

She held him by his scarf, but Abid peered out into the darkness where Ken was disappearing fast into the snow. With a quick nod to Bryony he shook himself free and slithered after him, and in a moment the snowstorm had swallowed the two figures. To Bryony's frustration they vanished into the night, taking their secret with them.

# Chapter Five

When Bryony arrived at school on Monday morning, she was puzzled to find the playground deserted.

She was also annoyed, because she was dying to talk to Abid. After several phone calls that weekend he had finally told her who he thought the beautiful woman in the gold, heart-shaped frame was. Bryony wasn't quite sure she believed him. If he was right, it would be incredibly cool, but it seemed too much of a coincidence. She was, however, open to persuasion.

Then she remembered why no one was about. Now that the Nativity play was less than two weeks away, Mrs Quigg had insisted on extra early-morning rehearsals. Bending to avoid the Christmas decorations, Bryony flew down the corridor as fast as her skates would carry her, and glided into the hall as inconspicuously as she could.

The atmosphere was tenser than ever. Mrs Quigg was playing some edgy scales and Abid, looking miserable, was on stage beside Jeremy and Shehzad, two of the smallest and shyest boys in the school. Shehzad was standing nervously in front of Jeremy with his back to him, and Jeremy was bent over with his arms round Shehzad's waist and the top of his head pressed against his bottom. As Bryony appeared, Abid motioned to the two boys to walk across the stage beside him. Both took a couple of steps, staggered, and fell over.

'It's no good, Mrs Quigg,' Abid sighed. 'We'll never make a donkey out of them.'

'*We have to*!' said Mrs Quigg, accompanying each word with a loud staccato note. 'I've hired the costume. Now – get up at once!'

Bryony gazed at Jeremy and Shehzad, the full horror of the situation dawning. 'Oh no, Mrs Quigg,' she pleaded. 'Not all the way to Bethlehem…'

Desperately, Bryony racked her brains. The thought of wearing tea towels and riding on the back of two small boys was quite unendurable.

'Couldn't I do it on skates?' she ventured wildly.

Bryony hadn't been very hopeful, but Mrs Quigg's reaction was even worse than she'd anticipated. Leaning forward with a strangled cry, she laid her head on the piano keys. A soft, despairing chord echoed round the hall. Then, at last, she straightened up.

'The Virgin Mary was great with child,' she told Bryony wearily. 'She *plodded* to Bethlehem. She did not glide. And she most certainly did not perform any spins, triple jumps, or pirouettes.

'Now, get yourself up on that donkey's back this instant, Bryony Bell,' she continued, 'and kindly remember we are no longer on Broadway.'

Defeated, Bryony took off her skates and climbed gingerly on top of Jeremy. Everyone wobbled precariously and Abid placed a steadying hand on Shehzad's head.

'So … *you've* been on Broadway, too, have you, Mrs Quigg?' he asked politely, with a wink at Bryony.

Mrs Quigg stopped mid-scale and the air in the hall seemed to freeze. 'As a matter of fact, Abid,' Mrs Quigg said quietly, 'I have.'

Suddenly Bryony realised the significance of Abid's question. 'Were you a singing star, Mrs

Quigg?' she asked, a shiver of excitement running up her neck.

Mrs Quigg nodded. Then, one by one, she removed the hairpins that held her purple waves in place and shook her head so that her hair cascaded down onto her shoulders. Everything was so quiet, you could have heard a snowflake land. Only a low moan of pain from Jeremy broke the silence.

'"The English Nightingale", they used to call me, on account of the sweet, liquid quality of my voice.' Mrs Quigg patted her hair. 'Titian, this was,' she told them. 'That's red. The kind of red the Italian artists loved to paint.' And she began to play a soft little melody.

Head still spinning, Bryony listened. The tune seemed familiar. Hadn't she heard Mr Undrum hum it? But before Bryony could think what it was, it stopped; and Mrs Quigg gazed forlornly into the distance.

'That song,' she sighed, 'is like a butterfly in the sky of my memory. Each time I feel it within my grasp, off it flutters once more. I just know it would make the perfect Big Number, but I fear I will never remember what it is. It's lost forever in the mists of time.'

Abid edged forward and looked down at Mrs Quigg. 'Have you any idea,' he said gently, 'what the song's about?'

'A star, Abid,' Mrs Quigg answered promptly. 'I know it's about a star. And a dream.'

She stared down at the piano keys as though they could unlock the secret.

'A dream…' she repeated, sighing again.

Still keeping his eyes on Mrs Quigg, Abid backed off till he was once more beside Bryony. Glowing with excitement, Bryony placed a foot gently but firmly on top of his. 'We've got to help her,' Byrony hissed. 'We've simply got to…'

Abid nodded solemnly. 'Whether she's the English Nightingale or not,' he hissed back, 'she's perilously close to breaking point.'

'Should we say something?' Byrony hissed again. But Abid shook his head.

'Not yet,' he said. 'Not till we're quite sure.'

The bell rang and Mrs Quigg, looking suddenly embarrassed, gave herself a shake. Sitting up straight, she pinned back her hair and glared at Mary, Joseph, and both halves of the donkey. 'Take it from where Joseph looks up at Mary, his eyes filled with a mixture of love and compassion,' she told them. 'And give it all you've got!'

'Ignore the bell,' she added crisply. '*This* is art.'

Suddenly determined to bring Mrs Quigg a shred of comfort in her hour of need, Abid turned to Bryony and gave her an intense look. 'Not much longer now, my love,' he said, his voice welling over with emotion like never before. 'For lo! I see the star ahead.'

That evening the sky was gunmetal grey as Bryony skated up the path to Big Bob's frost-encrusted potting shed. As she pushed open the door and saw him bent over his workbench in a warm little pool of light, her flagging spirits rose slightly.

'How's my princess?' he asked, sitting on his gold-padded tea chest and patting his lap. 'Things not so good?'

Bryony struggled not to wobble off Big Bob's knees. She stretched out her long legs and wiggled her Viper 3000s. The thought struck her that soon she'd be too tall to sit on her dad's lap. 'They've been better, Dad,' she admitted. 'Angelina's really getting me down, and the Nativity play's hit an all-time low.'

Big Bob gave Bryony a squeeze. 'Not always easy,' he said slowly, 'being the second oldest.'

Bryony looked down at him in surprise. 'How do you mean, Dad?' she asked. 'Angelina always thinks she's better than me. Being a singer and an actor and all that…'

Big Bob whistled thoughtfully through the gap in his front teeth. 'Is that how you see it, love?' he asked at last, and when Bryony nodded, he shook his head. 'Always looked up to you, Angelina has,' he said quietly. 'After all, lass – *all* the Bells 'cept us can sing. Angelina's not that special really, when you come to think about it.'

Bryony jumped off Big Bob's lap and stood facing him. She could hardly take in what he was saying.

'Our Angelina always felt you lumped her together with the other little 'uns,' Big Bob went on. 'Always wanted to do your own thing without her, you know.'

Bryony opened her mouth to protest, caught sight of Big Bob's sad blue eyes, and closed it again.

You had to admit, she suddenly thought, that there was some truth in what he'd said. But it had never occurred to her before that Angelina might want to be included in any of *her* plans. Come to think of it, the only time she and Angelina *had* got on well together was when they were both looking after Starburst. And now even that was gone. Hot tears began to roll down Bryony's cheeks. There was something oddly comforting about the feeling.

'Angelina looks up to me?' she breathed at last. 'Angelina *wants* to do things with me?' It sounded unbelievable, but Big Bob nodded.

'Thinks you're the bee's knees, Bryony,' he said gently. 'Though I'll grant you she's got some funny ways of showing it.'

The dinner gong echoed through the crisp air. Big Bob stood up and began to tidy away his tools. 'Told me she thinks it's a crying shame

**51**

you can't skate in that Nativity play, too,' he added. 'Though don't you be telling her I said that, or there'll be hell to pay.'

Bryony opened the potting shed door and peered out into the moonlit whiteness. Somewhere in the back of her mind, an idea was beginning to glimmer.

Angelina felt left out, did she?

Angelina wanted Bryony to include her in her plans, did she?

Well maybe – just maybe – there *was* something she and Angelina could do together! Something that urgently needed doing…

On the way towards the house, Big Bob pointed up at the sky. 'Just look at those stars, Bryony,' he said. And then, very softly, he began to hum.

Bryony stopped and spun round. She'd heard that tune – or the beginnings of it – today already.

'What are you humming, Dad?' she asked, and Big Bob laughed and stroked his moustache.

'Don't suppose it sounds much like it,' he said, 'but it was supposed to be the one Mr Undrum sang today at his Star Interview. On location, in Abid's conservatory.'

'Really, Dad?' Bryony said in surprise. 'You went along?'

Big Bob nodded. 'Trish wanted me to stand by with my screwdriver in case of emergencies.'

'But why was Mr Undrum singing?' Bryony asked.

'You'll find out tomorrow, lass,' Big Bob said, opening the door. 'When the first breakfast show goes on air. But, while I remember,' he added, stepping into the cosy kitchen, 'the song was called "When You Wish Upon A Star".'

Bryony watched Big Bob swing Little Bob up onto his shoulders and let him give his head three whacks with his hammer. But she didn't follow him inside. Instead she stayed on the doorstep, looking up again at the star-studded sky.

'"When You Wish Upon A Star"...' she repeated. 'That is it! Now all I need to do is get Angelina on my side, and we're in business.'

Being careful not to slip, Bryony threw her head back and performed a sedate but triumphant pirouette. As she spun, she picked out one star that was brighter than all the others and when she had stopped spinning she stared hard at it, crossed her fingers, and muttered something to herself.

And as Bryony made her wish she could have sworn that the star sprouted a tail, then shot off to make the wish come true.

# Chapter Six

'Breakfast with the Bells, opening titles, take *one*!'

Trish banged her clapperboard and everyone sat nervously at the breakfast table, waiting while the theme music played. As it faded, Trish signalled them to begin.

'Forget the cameras,' she had told them beforehand. 'What we want is normal chat, OK?'

The cameras began to roll. An uneasy silence descended. Then everyone began to speak at once. Only Bryony and Angelina, on opposite sides of the table, and with a wall of cereal packets between them, said nothing.

'Can't wait to see Bryony and Angelina in the Nativity play, can you, Melissa?' Melody said, with a winning smile at camera one.

'Absolutely, Melody,' Melissa replied, giving her a nudge under the table. 'I'll bet Bryony's a beautiful Virgin Mary!'

'Though you can't help thinking, can you,' Melody went on, 'that it'd be better if Angelina was Mary, because Angelina can *act*...'

'But of course Bryony can't be the angel, can she,' they chorused, pressing their identical heads together so they fused in a mass of gel, 'because Bryony *can't sing*!'

They stared expectantly from Bryony to Angelina, hoping for a reaction. Angelina pursed her lips into a magnificent pout, took a swipe at her boiled egg, decapitated it, and plunged her spoon in. A volcano of egg yolk erupted, and she glared down at the flow.

Miserably, Bryony squeezed the milk out of her sodden cornflakes with the back of her spoon. She was aware that camera two was looming, waiting for a close-up on another Angelina-Bryony mega-row. But Angelina, her cheeks glowing red with pent-up fury, refused to rise to Melody and Melissa's bait. The tension in the air could have sliced through a hard-boiled egg.

Suddenly Bryony stood up and held one finger in the air. Staring straight at Angelina, she spoke. 'As a matter of fact,' she announced dramatically, '*Angelina and I* have come up with a fantastically fabulous, humungously heavenly plan that's going to launch Mrs Quigg's Nativity play into the stratosphere.'

She paused dramatically, and Trish signalled to camera one to move in for a close-up.

Angelina's egg spoon landed in the middle of the yellow lava pool. Melody and Melissa dropped their marmaladen toasts sticky-side-down. Emmy-Lou's jaw dropped so far it landed in her Krispy Kubes. Little Bob, who had been about to hammer the top back on the honey jar, stopped mid-swing, and Big Bob, who had maintained a dignified silence till now, muttered, 'That's my girl!' under his breath.

Only Clarissa kept her cool. 'Really, Bryony?' she said. 'And what would that plan be?'

'Top secret I'm afraid, Mum,' Bryony said mysteriously. 'Let's just say that this year there's going to be more Christmas surprises than usual.'

She leaned across the table and carefully parted Angelina's braids. Then she put her nose as near to her sister's as she dared. 'What do you say, Angelina?'

All the Bells watched in suspense. For a few long moments, Angelina said nothing. Then, slowly, her pout began to disappear and very quietly she repeated: 'A fantastically fabulous, humungously heavenly plan?'

Bryony backed off a little and nodded.

'You want *me* to help you with a fantastically fabulous, humungously heavenly plan?' Angelina asked again, blushing furiously.

'You betcha, Angelina,' Bryony replied. 'Can't think of anyone better.'

Rather tentatively, Angelina rose from her seat. Only the soft *whirr* of camera one's close-up lens broke the silence.

'And there's absolutely no hypnotism involved?' she said cautiously.

'Absolutely, positively none,' Bryony assured her. 'But, with our combined talents, the result will be truly mesmerising.' And she held out her hand to her sister across the great cereal divide.

As if in a daze, Angelina leaned over and gave it a shy shake.

'Partners?' Bryony asked softly.

'Probably,' Angelina answered. 'Once I've heard the plan,' she added, not unreasonably.

Everyone took in a deep breath as Bryony pressed her lips close to Angelina's ear and whispered. In silent suspense they watched a tiny smile appear on Angelina's lips, and as the smile grew wider and wider and she nodded her head more and more enthusiastically, a huge sigh of relief filled the kitchen.

'Well!' breathed Clarissa as she scraped the egg yolk off Little Bob's forehead. 'Could this be Peace on Earth at last?'

Camera one panned out and swung to face Trish, who was scribbling on her clipboard and practically drooling with delight. 'Wow!' she gasped at the great British public. 'What *can* this fantastically fabulous, humungously heavenly plan be, I hear you ask? Only time will tell. But now,' she announced as she pushed the toaster aside to reveal a monitor screen, 'it's time for the very first Star Interview, which I filmed yesterday on location at the beautiful home of Dr and Mrs Ashraf.'

She turned to face the monitor. 'Here he is,' she went on dramatically, 'the *inexplicable*…

'…the *incomparable*…

'…the *utterly hypnotic* Ken Undrum, Man of Mystery!'

A series of bright-pink concentric circles whirled round the monitor screen and high-pitched, unearthly music played. Then, one by one, the circles disappeared, the music faded, and Ken Undrum came into focus.

The scene was Abid's conservatory. Steam swirled round Ken, who sat surrounded by tinsel-decorated palm trees, wearing a white suit with a red carnation in the buttonhole. He was sipping a bright-turquoise cocktail, and his red moustache had been waxed into points for the occasion. On his knee sat three white rabbits, one of which was delicately nibbling the carnation.

'Look!' Bryony whispered to Angelina. 'It's Lily!'

The camera switched to Trish, who was also looking exotic in a red sequined dress and matching beaded skullcap.

'Welcome, Ken,' she said. 'We're honoured to have you at our first Breakfast with the Bells Star Interview!'

Ken took a sip of his cocktail. 'Delighted, dear lady, I'm sure,' he smiled, as he dabbed his moustache with a pink silk handkerchief. 'Fire away.'

And the interview took off. Ken reminisced about his glory days on Broadway, describing vividly the spectacular illusions he and The Great Ronaldo had performed and, to Bryony's relief, he was careful not to mention hypnotism. Then the camera turned back to Trish.

'Broadway is certainly beckoning again, Ken,' she said earnestly. 'But I believe you have a very special reason for being back here in England?'

Beads of perspiration glistened on Ken's forehead. 'Indeed, Trish,' he nodded. 'For although my career is once more at its height…' he paused, picked up Lily, and kissed her pink nose, '…you see here before you a haunted man.'

'Do go on,' breathed Trish.

In answer, Ken stood up, closed his eyes and began to sing, and as the strains of the now-familiar song filled the kitchen, Bryony walked round to squeeze into Angelina's chair and clutch her arm. And, hidden from all cameras and prying eyes, Angelina clutched Bryony's arm too.

'*When you wish upon a star,*' Ken sang in his rich baritone voice.

'*Makes no difference who you are*
*When you wish upon a star*
*Your dream comes true…*'

Then he stopped, opened his eyes, and turned a tear-moist face to the camera.

'But alas,' he said, simply and sadly, 'my wish remains but a dream.'

There was a short silence. The screen became hazy, and in the background violins discreetly took up the melody of Ken's song.

Misty-eyed, Ken turned to camera and from his breast pocket he withdrew the little picture in its gold, heart-shaped frame. The faded image slowly expanded to fill the screen.

'It was on an evening like this, many, many years ago,' Ken said in dream-like tones, 'that I first set eyes on the woman who was to steal my heart forever. I was a young magician, just starting to make my name on the Broadway stage, and she…' he paused, overcome with emotion, and took a sip of his cocktail before continuing, '…she was Cornelia Merryweather,' he said at last. 'The English Nightingale.'

Bryony dug her nails so hard into Angelina's arm that Angelina winced.

'And that was her song.' Ken clutched Lily tightly to his breast. 'She was standing on a balcony above a rose garden, her Titian red hair glinting in the moonlight, singing in her sweet, liquid voice. Even the stars seemed to be listening. And…' he breathed finally, '…she broke my heart forever.'

'So…' Trish said carefully, '…things didn't work out?'

Ken's whole body was racked by a great sigh. 'Cornelia was as beautiful and as fragile as an English rose,' he said, replacing the picture in his pocket. 'But alas, not mine to pluck.'

'She was promised to another?'

Ken nodded into his glass. 'Engaged to an English banker,' he said sorrowfully. 'A much safer investment than a Man of Mystery. I wished upon a star that night,' he concluded softly, 'but the wish never came true.'

Angelina pressed her mouth close to Bryony's ear. 'But Mrs Quigg's name's Nell,' she hissed. 'I heard Mrs Ogilvie call her that.'

'It *has* to be her,' Bryony hissed back. 'The hair, the Nightingale, the song – you bet your life, Angelina. Mrs Quigg is Mr Undrum's lost sweetheart, or my name's not Bryony Bell.'

The monitor screen was fading back to the pattern of concentric circles, and a full orchestra had taken up the 'When You Wish Upon A Star' music. Bryony and Angelina whispered excitedly together as Trish brought the show to a close.

'But what about *Mr* Quigg?' Angelina said. 'Mr Undrum's got no chance if he's still around.'

'You've got a point there,' Bryony said thoughtfully. 'We need to find out if he's still on the scene before we spill the beans. *And* we need to be certain we've got the right Nightingale…'

The cameras pulled away for the final long shot of the waving Bells. The closing credits rolled, and Trish skipped delightedly round the table, hugging everyone in sight and telling them how absolutely fabulous they'd all been.

Bryony waved as enthusiastically as she could, but she was twitching with impatience. She couldn't wait to see Abid.

'You don't suppose Mrs Quigg watches breakast TV?' Angelina whispered.

'We'll know soon enough,' Bryony whispered back. 'Though somehow Mrs Quigg doesn't strike me as the breakfast-TV type.'

When the final tearful hug had been given, a very emotional Clarissa peeled herself away from Trish and shepherded the little 'uns off to get ready for school. 'So what *is* this Christmas surprise, Bryony?' she asked as she passed. 'We're all dying to know.'

But Bryony and Angelina shook their heads in unison. 'You'll have to wait till the Nativity play to find out,' Angelina said.

'We'll give you a clue though,' added Bryony tantalisingly. 'It's something *you* usually do!'

Clarissa considered this. 'Not going to sing 'Big Spender' in gold lamé frocks, are you?' she said at last.

But Bryony and Angelina only smiled mysteriously and shook their heads again.

# Chapter Seven

Later that morning, when Bryony and Abid took their places on stage, it was clear from her look of misery that Mrs Quigg had not seen Ken Undrum's romantic revelation.

Abid, however, had felt it wise to check, and asked politely whether she had seen the first Breakfast with the Bells show. Giving him a distracted look, Mrs Quigg had shaken her head then thumped down wearily on the piano stool.

'You can always tell by her hair when she's upset,' Abid whispered to Bryony as he gave her a leg-up onto Jeremy's back. 'Takes on a life of its own.'

Bryony took hold of Abid's tea towel and drew him close. 'You're *positive* there's no Mr Quigg?' she whispered urgently.

'I told you,' Abid whispered back. 'She's always saying "My late husband Nigel". That means he's passed away.'

'Then there's just the matter of her name…' Bryony said thoughtfully. 'We have to find out whether she really *was* Cornelia Merryweather.'

Mrs Quigg, who had been playing the opening number very softly, suddenly looked straight up at Bryony, and Bryony blushed.

'I trust,' she said nippily, 'that the donkey, the Virgin Mary, and the Virgin Mary's husband are ready to plod to Bethlehem without anyone sustaining major injury?'

Both parts of the donkey nodded as best they could and Abid gave Bryony his most compassionate look. Taking a large handful of Jeremy's jumper, Bryony gazed up to where Mrs Ogilvie had fixed a large, gold-foil star. The star had patterns cut out of it and a light inside. It was fixed to a length of rope, and a series of pulleys enabled it to lead the holy couple to their various ports of call. As the lights dimmed, it twinkled magically.

With the dimming of the lights, an eerie silence fell over the hall. Bryony glanced over to the wings, where Angelina was waiting for Mrs Quigg to play the introductory bars of the 'Wearily to Bethlehem' song.

But the introductory bars never came.

Bryony and Abid peered through the silent, starlit darkness. All that could be heard was a faint sniffing from the direction of the piano. Abid walked over to the edge of the stage and sat down.

'I've said it all along,' Mrs Quigg told him softly between sniffs. 'The show just doesn't work without a Big Number.'

Bryony heaved herself off Jeremy's back. Motioning to Angelina to follow her, she joined Abid. Tears now wracked Mrs Quigg's body.

'Every waking minute I have tried, but to no avail,' she sobbed. 'I simply cannot call that song to mind. It is almost as if I were forbidden ever to hear it again...'

Angelina gave Bryony a nudge. 'That's your Mr Undrum up to his tricks,' she whispered. 'Bet you any money he hypnotised her, all those years ago.'

Bryony looked admiringly at her. 'Of *course!*' she whispered back. 'You're a genius, Angelina.' Then she jumped off the stage. 'Cheer up, Mrs Quigg,' she said, with a knowing glance at Angelina. 'All you need to do is *wish upon a star...*'

For a fleeting second, recognition flashed over

Mrs Quigg's face and she seemed about to smile. Then, as quickly as it had appeared, the look was gone, leaving her even more sorrowful than before. 'I am afraid, Bryony,' she shook her head mournfully, 'it has to be faced. The show has no Big Number, and all the wishing in the world won't get it one.'

Abid stood up. Angelina and Bryony linked arms. All three smiled from ear to ear.

'OH, YES IT *HAS*!' they chorused, and as Mrs Quigg gazed up at them in complete bewilderment, Bryony whispered, 'You tell her.'

Angelina stepped forward, paused dramatically for a moment, then spoke.

'Bryony and me are going to give you a Big Number, Mrs Quigg,' she said sweetly. 'Bryony wrote the first verse this morning on the way to school.

'I'm going to help her write the rest,' she went on proudly, "cause Bryony says I've got a way with words, don't you, Bryony?'

Bryony nodded and patted Angelina's arm encouragingly. 'Now that we've got the tune,' she told Mrs Quigg, 'we're half-way there. That's what our mum always says.'

'Two Bells,' Abid pointed out, 'are better than one. Your Big Number's as good as written.'

'There's just one thing though,' Angelina continued, even more sweetly than before.

'A teensy-weensy alteration,' Abid added casually.

'Just a tweak...'

Angelina drew in breath. 'Bryony and me'd have to change parts,' she said, speaking very quickly. 'Bryony'd make a perfect angel in her

**71**

lovely white skating dress. And Abid and me'd do the Big Number as a duet.'

'Close two-part harmony,' Abid put in, wiggling his eyebrows seductively. 'It'll knock 'em dead!'

Bryony bit her lip as Mrs Quigg considered all this. The silence was broken by a soft thud as Jeremy fell over. 'Not so much strain on the donkey either,' Bryony pointed out. 'Angelina's lighter.'

'Like to hear the first verse, Mrs Quigg?' Abid said finally, leading Angelina to the centre of the stage, dusting Jeremy down, and settling her on his back. Then, in the clearest, purest, harmony, Abid and Angelina began to sing and as the last chord faded and the singers turned and bowed to their music teacher, Bryony leant over and whispered in her ear.

'And if you think *that's* good, just wait till you see my Multitude of the Heavenly Host on skates. The audience isn't going to know what hit them!' Then, with a wink to Angelina and Abid, she added, 'And of course, the whole thing'll be captured on camera…'

It took several minutes for all this to sink in, and Bryony, Abid and Angelina stood, fascinated, watching the change that came over Mrs Quigg as realisation dawned.

'On camera?' she breathed. A reddish glow began to brighten her cheeks. 'Wh- whatever do you mean?'

'Breakfast with the Bells,' Bryony said promptly. 'The show that's all set to "revolutionise the nation's breakfast time".'

'The producer wants the Nativity play to be the outside-broadcast Christmas special,' Abid went on. 'You'll be famous, Mrs Quigg.'

But Mrs Quigg seemed to have stopped listening. 'Your Big Number, Bryony…' she breathed. 'I'm sure that's the song that's lost in the mists of time… I'm sure that was *my* song…' And she gazed up at the twinkling golden star, her brow furrowed with the effort of remembering.

Bryony looked at Abid, and squeezed Angelina's hand. In reply, Abid smiled back and Angelina gave her an answering squeeze. 'Go on,' she whispered.

Bryony cleared her throat. 'Mrs Quigg,' she said nervously, 'does the name *Ken Undrum* mean anything to you? Because he's longing to meet you again.'

There was no reply, but the furrow on Mrs Quigg's brow cleared and a smile began to grow on her lips. Eyes still fixed skywards, she began to hum the 'When You Wish Upon A Star' melody. The more she hummed, the wider her smile became and as the last strains died, she spoke.

'Ken Undrum,' she whispered. 'Hearing that name again is like waking from a deep, deep sleep… "When You Wish Upon A Star" was *my* song,' she went on dreamily. Then, as much to herself as to Bryony, she added the magic words, 'It was *our* song…'

For a moment Bryony did not dare speak. Then, very softly, in case she broke the spell, she said, 'So you are Cornelia Merryweather?'

Mrs Quigg nodded. 'Nigel always felt Cornelia was a bit showy,' she explained. 'So, ever since we married, it's been plain old Nell. But now,' she said, closing the piano lid decisively, 'I do believe it can be Cornelia again.' She stood up and gazed starwards. 'I'd love to meet Ken again,' she murmured. 'And I'd love to meet him right here, under a star, with our song playing in the background, just like before. Do you think that might be possible?'

Bryony glanced at Abid and Angelina. Without a word, all three nodded. Then, misty-eyed, they gazed down at their music teacher's radiant face. And, for the next few silent moments, it was as though the years had slipped away and Nell Quigg was once more the English Nightingale smiling at her true love, under a starry Broadway sky.

# Chapter Eight

When Bryony and Angelina came home from school, the events of the day had made them unusually quiet.

Clarissa, who was busy handing out mince pies to everyone, gave them a curious look. 'You two all right?' she asked, and they nodded.

'Hunky-dory,' said Angelina.

'Never been better,' said Bryony.

Clarissa opened her mouth, then closed it rather impatiently. 'Won't waste my breath asking what's going on,' she said, opening the kitchen door and peering out at the blizzard that was raging. 'I'm sure all will be revealed in the fullness of time, and now I must feed your father before the potting shed's completely cut off from civilisation.'

Then, cradling Big Bob's mince pie lovingly to her breast, Clarissa set off.

'I'm going to give Melody and Melissa some

extra practice while I'm out,' she called back to Bryony and Angelina. 'Be darlings and do the chips, will you?'

Bryony tipped a load of potatoes into the sink. Angelina fetched a knife and a chopping board and waited patiently as Bryony began to peel. 'It's so *utterly* romantic, isn't it,' she said at last.

'Never seen anything *more* romantic,' Bryony agreed happily, handing Angelina a potato to chop.

'But shouldn't we tell Mr Undrum?' Angelina asked.

Bryony shook her head. 'Not till the day of the Nativity play,' she said decisively. 'If Mrs Quigg's got her heart set on meeting under a star with their song playing in the background, that's what Mrs Quigg's going to get.'

Angelina's face lit up. 'You're right,' she nodded. 'And I bet Trish'll love the surprise element.'

'What a TV moment!' Bryony agreed. 'And another thing,' she added as she plunged her scraper into the water with renewed vigour, 'Mr Undrum's always springing surprises on people. This time, *he'll* get the surprise of his life!' She handed some potatoes to Angelina.

'There's one thing that puzzles me, Bryony,' Angelina said. 'Why *did* Mr Undrum hypnotise Cornelia so she couldn't remember the song?'

'So she'd be spared the misery of thinking about her lost love,' Bryony explained solemnly. 'Poor Mr Undrum really thought she'd be better off with Nigel the banker, but he knew that secretly she'd always hanker after him.'

'I see...' said Angelina, thoughtfully quartering one of the potatoes. 'Mr Undrum knew that every time *he* heard the song he'd be dead upset, and he wanted to spare Cornelia the same pain.'

Bryony faced her sister squarely. 'Exactly,' she said. 'Mr Undrum meant well.'

She put down her potato scraper and braced herself. 'You know, Angelina,' she said, 'you really have misjudged Mr Undrum. Hypnotism isn't just about making people eat onions and gluing their hands together.'

Angelina frowned. 'What do you mean?'

'Well,' said Bryony carefully, 'hypnosis can help people. Have you noticed that Abid's asthma's gone?'

'Really?' said Angelina. 'Mr Undrum hypnotised it away?'

'You bet,' said Bryony. 'Five minutes with the old crystal pendulum, and now Abid's utterly wheeze-free.

'And another thing,' she added, crossing her fingers as she did, 'hypnotism can cure phobias.'

'Phobias?' Angelina said, baffled. 'What's phobias?'

'Really big fears,' Bryony told her, reaching into her pocket and taking out a piece of string threaded with a glass bead.

'Not as flashy as Mr Undrum's,' she said apologetically, 'but it does the trick.' And she began to swing the bead back and forth.

'A phobia...' Angelina repeated thoughtfully. 'But we don't know anyone who's got one of them, do we?'

There was a howl of wind as the door opened. Big Bob tumbled inside, pulled off his coat and shook snow all over Bryony, Angelina, and the pieces of potato.

'Chips – capital!' he smiled, rubbing his hands together. 'Your mum's digging the youngest *Broadway Belles* out of the music studio, girls, so I'll just go and have a nice hot bath.'

'Hang on,' said Bryony, grabbing him firmly by the strap of his dungarees. 'This will only take a moment, but it will change your life forever.'

Then she led him to the table, sat him down, and swung the glass bead back and forth in front of his nose. Angelina looked on anxiously.

'Follow the crystal,' Bryony intoned.

Obligingly, Big Bob obeyed.

'Now,' said Bryony, 'I want you to picture yourself on board a big aeroplane...'

Angelina gave a little gasp, but Big Bob's face was a picture of calm. 'Right you are, lass,' he said happily.

'You're flying all the way to the States,' Bryony continued, 'cruising at an altitude of 20,000 feet. But are you nervous?'

Big Bob, totally transfixed by Bryony's bead, continued to move his head from side to side. 'Not remotely,' he said at last.

'Are your palms clammy?'

'Not a bit of it,' Big Bob replied promptly. 'In fact,' he added, 'I'm rather enjoying it...'

'So you're not frightened?' Bryony asked, beginning to reduce the bead's momentum.

The sideways movements of Big Bob's head slowed too and finally came to rest. After a short consideration, he laughed. 'Frightened of flying?' he said. '*Moi*?'

'I am going to count to three and snap my fingers,' Bryony went on, staring hard into Big Bob's eyes, 'and when I do you will be wide awake; and you will never be afraid of flying again. One … two … three!'

At the final number, Big Bob leapt out of his seat. Then he grabbed the rhinestone-studded Stetson from the stuffed bear's head, put it on, slapped his thigh and yelled, 'Yee-hah!' just as the door opened and a very bemused Clarissa led the *Broadway Belles* in and began to remove her cloak.

'Clarissa, my angel,' Big Bob said ecstatically, sweeping her up, snow and all, and dancing round the kitchen with her in his arms. 'Come fly with me!'

Bryony lay in bed that night, going over everything that had happened. Her Viper 3000s hung in their usual place over the wardrobe doorknob, and as she pictured the white, feathery skating dress inside and imagined how even more wonderful it was going to look when Abid's mum had unpicked the silver star and embroidered on a gold-sequined shooting one, she felt ripples of excitement zing up and down her back. This was going to be the very best Christmas ever!

She looked at the Vipers again. There was, she thought, just one little problem. Compared to all the other problems she'd had lately, it was fairly minor. But still – it *was* a problem.

Her train of thought was broken by a soft knock at the door. Angelina tiptoed in and perched on the bed.

'Can't sleep either?' Bryony grinned.

'Written the second verse of the Big Number,' Angelina answered, pushing a piece of paper under her nose.

Excitedly, Bryony read. 'Wow, Angelina!' she said. 'This is just great. We'll have it written in no time!' She looked admiringly at her sister. 'Maybe you could sing it?'

'And maybe you could let me see how you'd skate it?' Angelina answered.

But Bryony did not move. Instead, she traced her finger solemnly round the pink flowers on her duvet cover. 'I'd love to,' she said. 'It's just…' She swung her legs off the bed, went over to the wardrobe, and unhooked the Vipers. Then she sat back down and stroked their white composite uppers. 'It's these,' she said at last. 'They nip.'

'But you'll be able to do the play in them?' Angelina asked anxiously. 'Won't you?'

Bryony shrugged. 'Sure,' she said. 'As long as I don't wear socks. But they're not going to last much longer, Angelina. And it seems like it was only yesterday that I got them.'

'You need new rollerskates, Bryony,' Angelina said gently.

Bryony nodded. 'Reckon Mum and Dad'll get me them for Christmas?'

'Sure to,' Angelina smiled. 'After all, you got us the big contract, didn't you!'

Bryony stroked her skates again. 'I'll ask for another pair of Vipers,' she said, cheering up. 'Can't get skates better than Vipers, that's for sure!'

She pulled them on with difficulty and struck a pose by the dressing table. 'Make way for the angel's entrance!' she announced. Then she did a magnificent leap right across the bedroom, landed as softly as stardust, bowed her head and said in an uncannily awe-inspiring voice, 'Behold, I bring you great good news!'

Angelina could hardly contain herself. 'It's wonderful, Bryony!' she said. 'Looks just like you're flying.'

Bryony curtsied, winced slightly, and eased the Vipers off. Angelina surveyed Bryony's red and blistered feet. Then, very thoughtfully, she said goodnight and tiptoed off to her own bedroom...

# Chapter Nine

Next morning Bryony woke earlier than usual. The house was so silent it felt as though a thick layer of snow was muffling every single sound, and for a while she lay in her cosy warm bundle of bedclothes, waiting happily for the day to begin.

Usually Bryony was the first Bell to get up, so when she heard a little sound from the landing she thought she must have been imagining things. Then it came again – a tiny creak, like someone trying to walk without making a noise. And then a rustle. A *distinct* rustle…

Bryony eased herself quietly out of bed and tiptoed over to the door. Making sure she didn't squeak, she opened it a crack and peeped out just in time to see Angelina's holly-patterned fleecy pyjamas disappearing in the direction of the staircase.

Odd, Bryony thought, Angelina usually stayed in her bed till the last possible moment... Bryony slipped out of her room and followed the pyjamas to the head of the stairs.

'Angelina!' she called out in as loud a whisper as she dared. But Angelina didn't answer. Instead she scurried on down, and as she rounded the bend at the bottom Bryony clearly saw her stuff a very large roll of paper down her front.

Intrigued, Bryony walked back to her bedroom. There was something very suspicious about Angelina's behaviour, and normally Bryony would have charged after her and demanded to know what was going on. But right now things between them were at an all-time high. It would be a shame to risk spoiling their new-found friendship.

Still deep in thought, Bryony dressed and went downstairs. Cautiously, she opened the kitchen door and immediately Angelina, who had been looking out of the kitchen window, wheeled round and blushed crimson.

'Good morning, Angelina,' Bryony said politely, trying her best not to look at Angelina's trouser leg from which a roll of paper was protruding. 'Nice to see you following the old

Duty Rota again.'

'Ah … yes,' Angelina stammered, grabbing a couple of mugs and a milk jug with one hand and flinging them with some difficulty onto the kitchen table. 'The Duty Rota … of course…'

Bryony lunged forward and caught the milk jug as it rolled across the table. 'Everything OK?' she said.

'A-1 OK,' Angelina replied promptly, walking very stiffly past Bryony and into the living room. 'Just looking out for Trish,' she added, pulling back the curtain and breathing on the frost patterns. 'Can't wait for filming to start…'

Determined not to show her suspicions, Bryony went on setting the table. A few bumps and coughs from above indicated that the rest of the family was beginning to stir. Then the doorbell rang, but when Bryony rushed out to open it, her way was barred by Angelina.

'That'll be Trish and the camera crew. I'll get it, Bryony!' she insisted. And when Bryony still hovered in the hall, she added, 'Why don't you go and round the little 'uns up? We don't want to be late starting now, do we?'

Reluctantly, Bryony did as she was told. But instead of climbing the stairs she crouched down behind the banister and listened. Quite distinctly, she heard Angelina hiss, 'Quick, Trish – while Bryony's out of the way!' Then the living room door was closed and there was silence.

Bryony climbed the stairs slowly, and by the time she reached the landing, the Breakfast with the Bells theme music had begun. No sooner had the first bars rung out than every bedroom door opened and a blur of Bells shot past her, heading excitedly for their second morning of TV stardom.

Bryony sighed and went into her bedroom. What was Angelina up to *now*? she wondered, as she sat at her dressing table and fastened her hair into two bright bunches with a pair of mistletoe hair ties. She was behaving very oddly…

'You nearly ready, Bryony love?'

Bryony jumped as she caught sight of Big Bob's reflection. 'Sure, Dad,' she said, unhooking her Vipers and swinging them round her shoulders. 'Mustn't miss our cue – come on!'

She led the way out but, to her surprise, Big Bob seemed in no hurry to be on set. In fact, he positively *ambled* along the landing and when he got to the top of the stairs he sat down and motioned to Bryony to sit beside him.

'Got any thoughts about what you'd like Santa to bring you this Christmas, lass?' he said conversationally, and as he did he nudged Bryony's shoulder so that the toe-stops of her Vipers dug in hard. ''Cause you know how sometimes Santa's little elves need a bit of advance warning, if you get my drift?' he added, with a broad wink.

The theme music had stopped now. Bryony bit her lip. It was the ideal opportunity to ask for new Vipers, but somehow it didn't feel right. 'I really think we ought to get to the kitchen, Dad,' she said worriedly. 'What's Trish going to think if there are two Bells missing?'

But Big Bob waved his hand dismissively. 'Don't always have to do everything bang on cue,' he said. 'After all, we're supposed to act natural, aren't we?' And he settled down comfortably on the stair as though time was no object.

'Oh, well,' said Bryony, relaxing too, 'if you're sure it's OK, then there *is* something I might like Santa's little elves to think about...'

Later that week, Bryony settled beside Abid in

the wings to await the arrival of the Virgin Mary on stage and, as her eyes grew accustomed to the dark, she couldn't believe what she saw. Instead of his brown dressing gown and Irish-linen tea towel, Abid now sported a shiny, grey salwar kameez with gold trim.

'Wow...' she whistled. 'Looks like Shabana Ashraf, Designer to the Stars, has been on your case!'

Abid nodded rather glumly. 'Couldn't keep her away once she knew it was going to be televised,' he said. 'Her pinking shears haven't stopped snipping!' He smoothed down the kameez, which sprang stiffly up again. 'Personally, I was happier in the dressing gown. Somehow this doesn't look like a garment that's been across a desert…'

Then he nodded in the direction of the opposite wings. 'Wait till you see the Virgin Mary,' he muttered, as a vision of pale-blue iridescent loveliness shimmered back and forth in the gloom. 'Mum says it's "demure, with a hint of glamour",' he added. 'Personally, I think it's too glitzy by half, but Mrs Quigg loves it, so there you are.

'Mind you,' he added, 'she's loving *everything* these days!'

Bryony stood up, smoothed down her skating dress, and prepared for her entrance. The Virgin Mary, however, was still at the side of the stage fiddling with her white satin headdress and looked nowhere near being ready for the visitation.

As Mrs Quigg played a more than usually jaunty version of her angel-wings music, Bryony moved close to Abid. 'Angelina's up to something,' she whispered. 'Did you notice me and Dad made a late entrance this morning?'

Abid nodded. 'Thought you were never coming,' he said.

Bryony looked at him warily. Why was he refusing to meet her eye?

'So,' she went on as coolly as she could, 'what did they talk about when we weren't there?'

Abid pulled at a thread in his kameez. 'Just chat,' he said quickly. 'Absolutely nothing.'

A couple of extra-loud tinkles from the piano announced the long-awaited arrival of the Virgin Mary in all her glory, and as Angelina delivered her lines flawlessly and with immaculate expression, Bryony pulled Abid closer. 'Not hiding anything from me, are you, Abid?' she said, looking deep into his brown eyes.

'Me?' Abid replied indignantly. 'Would I do a thing like that, Bryony?'

Feeling somewhat comforted, Bryony pushed off and glided into the starlight. Then she flapped her wings and rose into the air. But as she landed in a perfect arabesque at the Virgin Mary's feet it occurred to her that Abid had not actually answered her question…

The following days simply whizzed by in a flurry of rehearsals and breakfast shows, and before you could say 'Jingle Bells' it was the day before the Nativity play performance and just four days before Christmas.

When Trish arrived for the morning's filming she was wearing a pair of brown-felt reindeer antlers with tiny golden bells, and looked particularly flushed and elated. 'Take a look at this,' she announced as she tipped the contents of a large bin bag onto the table. 'Fan mail!'

With shouts of delight everyone pounced on the letters, excitedly searching for ones that were personally addressed to them. They were thrilled with what they read.

Three boys in Wolverhampton had voted Angelina Pout of the Year. A whole class of six year olds from Aberystwyth wanted Emmy-Lou to make a celebrity visit to their sponsored tap dance. A shinty team in Belfast had won their first game of the season after adopting Little Bob as their mascot, and had sent him his very own shinty stick on which they had written 'You fixed it for us!' And, from Land's End to John o' Groats, girls clamoured for advice from Melody and Melissa on how to deal with their split ends.

The grown-ups hadn't been left out either. There was a very appreciative letter from a joiner in Grimsby telling Big Bob he'd never seen a better-constructed kitchen cabinet in all his born days; and a host of requests for fashion tips, plus two rather doubtful proposals of marriage, for Clarissa.

But the biggest, sparkliest pile of fan mail by far was for Bryony! From all corners of the country, letters had flooded in as girls and boys sent her photos of themselves in their skating gear and begged her to tell them the secret of her success.

'Reckon you're on your way to your very own fan club, lass,' Big Bob grinned at Bryony, and Bryony turned to camera one and promised everyone who had written a personal reply.

'So keep those letters coming, folks!' Trish urged. Then, reaching into one of her pockets, she took out a little bundle of envelopes. 'Remember that fabulous Star Interview when Ken Undrum told us about his long-lost love, Cornelia Merryweather?' she said, fanning out the bundle. 'Just look at this! We've been *inundated* with letters from English Nightingales all over the country!' She opened some of the envelopes and held several photos up to the cameras.

'Amazing, isn't it,' Big Bob remarked under his breath to Clarissa, 'how many women of a certain age've got Titian red hair…'

'Apparently,' Trish went on delightedly, 'there's 14 in London, five in Doncaster, seven in Glasgow and one in Bristol – all *dying* to meet Ken again!

'So, folks,' she said with a wink to camera one, 'don't miss the Breakfast with the Bells Christmas special! What a line-up we've got for you...' She paused dramatically. 'We'll join the Bells live as they eat their Christmas breakfast. Then we'll bring you our very first outside-broadcast special,' she continued, her voice rising higher and louder. 'That's none other than Bryony, Angelina and Abid, in the Nativity play to end all Nativity plays!'

Sandwiched between Big Bob and Clarissa, Bryony listened with growing excitement, and when Trish dropped her voice confidentially and added, 'And, believe me, there'll be a few Christmas surprises in store!' she glanced over at Angelina and gave her a little wink.

Angelina winked back, and Bryony heaved a sigh of relief. Everything, it appeared, was all right after all...

# Chapter Ten

Bright and early on Christmas morning, an excited bevvy of Bells sat at the breakfast table with mugs of tea and warm mince pies. The kitchen was garlanded with holly and tinsel, and looked incredibly festive. Trish was looking festive too in a short, red-sequined Santa suit and matching hat, with flashing Rudolf the Red Nosed Reindeer earrings.

'Hi, folks, and welcome!' she announced gaily to camera one. 'The Bells sure are ringing out for Christmas today! And, as we promised you,' she went on as fake snowflakes began to fall from netting above their heads, 'today's Christmas special is packed full of surprises. And the first one happened at Peachtree Primary School just three days ago…'

Trish pointed over to a mistletoe-bedecked monitor. Everyone watched the screen with bated breath as the 'When You Wish Upon A

Star' music played, and Mrs Quigg appeared at the piano in a figure-hugging, black evening dress, her hair cascading over her shoulders in glorious Titian red waves and her cheeks glowing rose-pink.

'The look of love…' whispered Clarissa to Big Bob, and Big Bob blushed and nodded.

'We've all been there…' he whispered back.

Everyone, except Angelina, glued themselves to the screen. Bryony looked sideways at her. Why was she so fidgety?

The scene opened on a starlit hillside, and as three shepherds watched several cardboard sheep, the camera panned round the audience. There they all were! Clarissa and Mrs Ashraf, both looking entrancing; Big Bob and Dr Ashraf, handkerchiefs at the ready; Melody and Melissa in matching muffs, Emmy-Lou looking as though she had dropped off a Christmas tree; Little Bob, very grown-up in a velvet suit and matching bow tie. And, at the end of the row, his eyes glued to the vision on the piano stool, Ken Undrum in a midnight-blue suit with a red rose in his buttonhole.

Then, just as the shepherds settled down to sleep, the doorbell rang and, as though she had been expecting it, Angelina jumped up and ran out of the kitchen. Bryony got up and tried to follow her, but immediately found herself sandwiched tightly between Melody and Melissa.

Defeated, Bryony sat down and turned her attention back to the screen where, any minute now, the audience would be transported to the humble carpenter's workshop, which had been specially kitted out by Big Bob himself.

There was a gasp of delight as the Virgin Mary drifted on stage in her pale-blue shimmering finery, and delivered her lines more professionally than ever before. Then, at last, Mrs Quigg's angel-wings music played.

Bang on cue, Bryony soared through the air to land, gentle as cotton wool. Before announcing her tidings of great good news, she wove her way between the piles of saws and hammers and mounds of wood shavings, looking as mystical as any angel should. Then, trying not to flinch at the pain, she rose up on her points, indicated the star, and set off to tell the shepherds to gather up their lambs and follow it wherever it might lead.

There was a pregnant pause as the lights dimmed. The opening bars of the Big Number rang out and, with scarcely a wobble, the grey fur-fabric donkey entered with the Virgin Mary on its back and a very concerned Joseph at its head.

And that was when Bryony got her first Christmas surprise. For not only was Abid on screen, he was suddenly also there in the kitchen, wearing a red–and–gold salwar kameez and carrying a big gold-wrapped box. 'Happy Christmas, everyone!' he said, handing the box to Angelina.

Bryony felt a tiny wince, not unlike when her Vipers nipped. There was, she thought, no doubt Abid and Angelina had been getting on like a house on fire since they'd been playing the holy couple. He'd even begun to enjoy acting. Now, all those looks of love and concern must have borne fruit…

Trying hard to bite back tears, Bryony watched Angelina head for the Christmas tree with the beautiful box.

'Sssssssh!' ordered Clarissa as everyone moved along to let Abid sit down. 'This is Bryony and Angelina's Big Number, and we've got to hear every syllable!'

Silence descended on the kitchen, and Abid and Angelina began their duet.

'*When the journey's far too far,*' they sang.
'*And you wonder where you are*
*If you wish upon a star*
*Your dream comes true*'

The donkey plodded over to the first of a series of inn doors, each of which Abid knocked. Then, shaking his head sadly, he sang the next verse as a solo:

'*Even though they lock each door*
*Even though our feet are sore*
*Keep on wishing on a star*
*It WILL come true*'

Bryony bit her lip, then sighed with relief as the donkey made the difficult manoeuvre through the door of the friendly innkeeper, in whose stable Abid helped Angelina dismount. The star rose jerkily on its cable till it twinkled down on them and, holding hands, they sang the third verse:

'*In a strange and far-off land*
*Help, at last, will be at hand*

*If you wish upon a star*
*Your dream comes true'*

Then, exhausted, Angelina sank onto the straw. A scuffle followed as the donkey sidestepped round to cover the actual moment of childbirth, and then the camera panned in for a close-up of the holy child cradled in his mother's arms.

From the kitchen table, a chorus of sniffs rang out as the Virgin Mary and Joseph gazed tenderly down at their offspring and sang the last verse:

'*One day when our son is tall*
*We'll tell him, "When you were small*
*And we wished upon a star..."*'

The piano accompaniment slowed as the couple stood up, held the holy infant aloft so that his little plastic form was silhouetted against the golden star, and slowly and softly sang:

'*"Our dream ... came ... true!"*'

The applause that rang out at the end was not

as loud as the crowds on Broadway had been; but as Bryony listened to it again, and saw the close-ups of her tearful family, she knew she had never, ever, felt so proud.

The 'When You Wish Upon A Star' music rose to a crescendo. A red heart filled the screen.

'But that isn't the only dream that came true this Christmas,' Trish's excited voice-over announced. 'We've all been following the story of Ken Undrum and his long-lost love, Cornelia Merryweather...' she continued. 'Well, folks... here's the moment they were reunited!'

There was a drum roll, and the inside of the heart melted to reveal Mrs Quigg rising in slow motion from the piano stool. Then it panned round to Ken Undrum who walked towards her and flung his arms around her. Oblivious to the shouts of 'Encore!' they embraced rapturously and gazed into one another's eyes.

'Ken...' breathed Mrs Quigg.

'Cornelia...' breathed Ken.

'At last,' they both breathed, 'our dream has come true!'

As Ken and Cornelia's lips met, the heart re-formed to draw a red veil over their kiss and the screen slowly turned black.

Trish stood up and beamed at camera one. 'So there you are, viewers,' she said, 'our first Christmas surprise. And the happy couple are now celebrating their engagement in a luxury Broadway hotel, courtesy of Channel 4! But there's another surprise,' Trish went on, waving a piece of paper at the camera, 'in the shape of this *film contract*. A top American film-maker has been watching Breakfast with the Bells and reckons they're movie stars in the making! So next year the show will be shot on location in…' She paused dramatically. '*HOLLYWOOD!*'

The kitchen exploded in a series of whoops and cheers and yee-hahs as the Bells hugged each other, and congratulated each other, and danced round in one another's arms. And, in all the merriment, there was no one who whooped and cheered and yee-hah'd more loudly or more joyfully than Big Bob.

They were making so much noise that not even Bryony noticed Angelina slip into the living room and go over to the Christmas tree. All eyes were still on Trish, for Trish was making yet another curious announcement.

'But the surprises aren't over yet,' she was saying. 'Before we say goodbye and wish you all a Happy Christmas, here's a flashback to Angelina Bell's special Christmas appeal, which viewers will remember we filmed last week, when Bryony was safely out of the way...'

Bryony hardly knew where to look. On the screen, her sister's face beamed out at her and in the kitchen Angelina stood right in front of her, holding the golden box.

'Hi!' said the on-screen Angelina. 'Here's a Christmas challenge for all you rollerskate makers out there!' And she unfurled a large roll of paper on which she had drawn a pair of rollerskates. But what rollerskates! Bryony's heart did a triple-flip as Angelina pointed out all the features she had designed.

'I call them Bryony 3000s,' she explained. 'They're white, of course, but they've got *gold* wheels, and a *gold* logo, which is Bryony's face, and when you skate really fast...' she pointed to the back of the golden wheels, '...little stars shoot out! So I'm really hoping,' she said with an alluring look to camera, 'that someone out there can make a pair of size four Bryony 3000s in *double-quick time*, for my sister's Christmas. Because,' she added, 'I think she's the biggest star of us all!'

All of a sudden, Bryony's entire world seemed to catapult into outer space as Angelina thrust the golden box into her arms. 'Happy Christmas, Bryony,' she said. 'I hope you like them.'

Camera one zoomed in for a close-up of the unwrapping. Everyone jostled for a view. Speechless, Bryony removed the gold tissue paper, held the skates up, then slipped them on.

The Bryony 3000s were a perfect fit. Their leather was whiter and softer and shinier than the snow on the potting shed roof. Their wheels were as gold as the Christmas star. And, very best of all, above the glittering Bryony 3000 logo, Bryony's own face, her favourite rose hair ties picked out in tiny red stones, sparkled out.

Bryony looked round the sea of faces till she came to Big Bob's. He was standing squashed up against the stuffed bear's head and when he met her gaze he reached up, took off the rhinestone-studded Stetson, and hurled it to land right on her head. 'Come on, princess!' he called. 'Let's see if you can make the stars come out!'

Head buzzing with happiness, Bryony pushed off and, followed closely by camera two, skated three times round the living room, finishing off

with a triple spin that sent showers of stars onto
the carpet.

'Oh, thank you, Angelina!' she said, hugging
her sister. 'They couldn't be more perfect.'

She took Angelina's hand and pulled her back into the kitchen, where Clarissa was handing out lemonade to the children and Big Bob was carefully balancing a little silver tray of glasses filled with pink champagne.

'There you are, lass,' he winked. He handed Bryony the smallest champagne glass, and watched as she took her first tentative sip.

'Thanks, Dad,' she said, feeling a lovely rosy glow. 'Makes me feel really grown-up.'

As a starburst of champagne bubbles shot up her nose, Bryony looked down at the sea of happy faces. The Bryony 3000s made her feel even taller than before. In fact, she thought with sudden surprise, she was almost as tall as Trish now.

It was a giddy, sparkly feeling, like flying. She did a spin, and the Bryony 3000s sent out another starry spray.

'What was the wish you wished on the star, Bryony?' Angelina had squeezed in close and was whispering in her ear. 'Was it for new skates?'

Bryony began to shake her head. Then, catching Big Bob's eye, she stopped.

'Let's just say,' she said, giving Angelina a hug, 'that whatever it was, *you* made it come true.'

The kitchen exploded into even more cheers and, above the hubbub, Big Bob banged the table for silence. Then he raised his glass in Bryony's direction.

'A special Christmas toast,' he announced, as camera one zoomed in for a final, rather wobbly, close-up, 'to our Bryony – the star who makes *all* our wishes come true.'

# About the Author

I was born in Stranraer, a small town by the sea in Galloway, and I still like to be there as much as I can. I love the sea, the lochs and the rivers.

Most of the time, though, I live in Glasgow with my cats Lily, and Lily's son The Woozle. When I'm not writing, I teach English as an Additional Language at Glendale Primary School. The children I teach are almost always the inspiration for my characters.

I enjoy reading, drawing, making shadow puppets, gardening, and listening to music. I also play treble recorder in the Scottish Recorder Orchestra. I spend a lot of time practising! The Bryony books are fun to write because they give me the chance to write songs.

I have had 14 books published. These include *Speak Up, Spike!*, *Shadowflight* and *The Pen-pal from Outer Space*, all of which were named Guardian Book of the Week. My first picture book came out this year, it's called *Starting School*.

I've really enjoyed writing the *Bryony Bell* books, and getting to know more and more about the characters. In this book I wanted to give Mrs Quigg a star part, and I hope her 'glitzy' past will be as nice a surprise for readers as it was for Bryony and Abid.

I wonder what the future will hold for Bryony and the *Broadway Belles*. I'm sure they'll go from strength to strength. What do you think? If you'd like to see a bit more of Bryony, look at my website:

www.alchemywebsite.com/franzeskaewart

# Time
## AND AGAIN

## Rob Childs

*"By a click of the clock, You can go in reverse,
Time and Again, For better or worse."*

With the discovery of a strange-looking
watch, twins Becky and Chris gain the
power to travel back in time. It's the
opportunity to relive events and put things
right. But trying to change the past doesn't
always work out as the twins intend.
Especially when class troublemaker
Luke is around…

# Black Cats
## Books to pounce on